How to use t

In this magic book, the solutions to each problem are secretly hidden under silver circles. Answer all the subtraction problems, then, to check your answers, scratch the silver circles with a coin. The solutions will magically appear!

Have fun!

17-9=.....

29-21=.....

73-13=.....

39-27=.....

26-12=.....

20-11=.....

59-6=.....

55-25=.....

Solve the subtraction problems and write your answer on the dotted lines. Check your answers by scratching the silver circles with a coin.

47-31=.....
50-18=.....
43-15=.....
32-8=.....
23-17=.....
68-16=.....
39-28=.....
24-16=.....
50-14=.....
46-13=.....
28-6=.....
60-32=.....

93-24= .....

87-31= .....

98-15= .....

92-16= .....

99-38= .....

72-15= .....

100-28= .....

67-36= .....

Solve the subtraction problems below and write the difference of each step on the dotted lines. Then check your answers.

100 → -12 → ..... → -24 → ..... → -17 → ..... → -39 → .....

75 → -27 → ..... → -11 → ..... → -8 → ..... → -15 → .....

97-38= .....

Solve all the subtraction problems in the bubbles and show which answer matches the number on the treasure chest.

Solve all the subtraction problems on the snake and check your answers.

Solve all the subtraction problems on the leaves and check your answers. Which answer matches the number on the leaf in the parrot's beak?

94-16=.....

48-9=.....

85-9=.....

81-5=

.....

77-8=.....

63-5=.....

70-16=.....

Solve the subtraction problems on the walls of the museum and find the answer which is the same as the number on Sarah's map.

72 (-19) ..... (-24) ..... (-12) .....

45 (-7) ..... (-10) ..... (-4) ..... (-8) .....

64 (-8) ..... (-11) ..... (-7) ..... (-15) .....

Solve the subtraction problems on the floor of the museum and write the difference of each step on the dotted lines. Then check your answers.

Solve the subtraction problems on the palm trees and check your answers. Draw a line to match each of your answers to the dolphin with the corresponding number.

87-62-9=.....
77-19-40=.....
65-8-51=.....
78-33-6=.....
87-8-7=.....
99-19-75=.....
72-56-9=.....
SOS
7
5
31
17

Solve the subtraction problems on the walls and circle the correct difference.
Then check your answers.

75-49= 26 / 27

94-65= 28 / 29

99-74= 24 / 25

74-16= 58 / 59

67-39= 27 / 28

90-27= 63 / 64

50-37= 12 / 13

36-16= 20 / 21

82-15= 67 68
93-27= 65 66
49-25= 23 24
Solve the subtraction problem below by subtracting from 100 the number of lions and the number of birds which are drawn on the wall. Then check your answers.
100- ..... - ..... = ...
58-34= 24 25

Solve the subtraction problems on each rock and check your answers. Which difference matches the number found above the erupting volcano?

Solve the subtraction problems found on the lava and check your answers.

16
71-52= .....
32-18= .....
78-..... = 13
.....-45= 39
100-..... = 58
.....-43= 44
90-..... = 71
.....-8= 23
88-..... = 55
33-15= .....
51-..... = 40
.....-19= 65
92-..... = 35
92-..... = 50
.....-32= 9

Find the missing numbers in the following subtraction problems and write your answers on the dotted lines. Then check your answers.

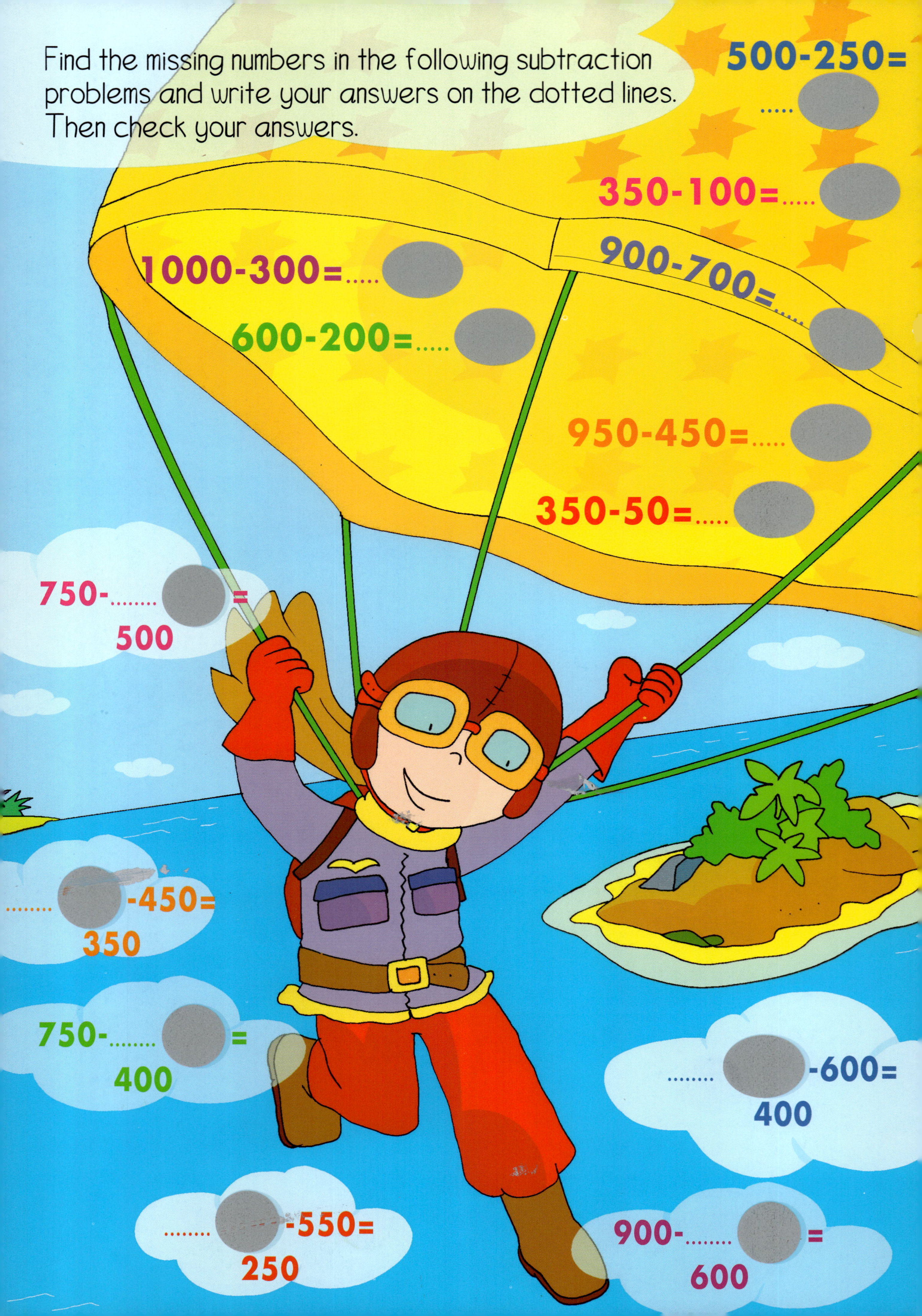

500-250= .....

350-100= .....

1000-300= .....

900-700= .....

600-200= .....

950-450= .....

350-50= .....

750- .... = 500

.... -450= 350

750- .... = 400

.... -600= 400

.... -550= 250

900- .... = 600